Proper Dragon Tales No.3

Secret of the Standing Stones

Words and Pictures by Caroline Downey

The artwork in this book is available as prints.

This book is dedicated to all those who believe in Dragons

The Black Mountains is a popular place for walking and provides spectacular views from the famous Offa's Dyke Path as it passes along Hatterrall Hill to Hay Bluff. Near this route is a mysterious location, not easily found. There was nothing unusual about the circular clearing in the heather; until a local historian explained that centuries ago this was once a place where huge standing stones dominated the landscape. Although not knowing precisely what purpose this site served, it probably had a sacred link from Celtic times and a romantic suggestion is that it could have been a connection point between this and the other world.

As I stood on the edge of the circle, I really felt a strange power while others with me heard sounds – I did not dare to step into the area.

This account of the standing stones inspired my third Proper Dragon Tale and includes the escapades of a greedy goat – and growing up with them, I know how crafty a goat can be.

Artist/Author Caroline Downey

I be the one who tells

I have always lived amongst the rugged countryside of the Black Mountains where it is easy for a dragon like me to exist, undiscovered. The steep mountains throw shadows over my lovely valley, preventing modern communication links with the outside world – and that's just how I like it. Living is good and honest but sometimes maybe a little mischievous; nevertheless it adds to the fun of things.

For centuries I have been surveying my patch, watching the ways of creature and folk as I fly over my pleasant land, though I do be careful not to go too near the Greedy Giant Mountain who sleeps at the bottom of my valley, as he might wake and eat me up. Legend says he is full of dragons – no wonder I am the last of my kind.

Many a mystery my mountains hold, only I know those happenings that can be told — now that reminds me of an adventure about a goat called Gwillim. He had a challenging time when discovering a strange place on one of my mountains and if you care to listen I might just be the one who tells you a Proper Dragon's Tale.............

So cwtch up and step into my pages.

Secret of the Standing Stones

On this morning, the autumn mist settles gently over my land, exposing just the rocky peaks of the Black Mountains. Looking down, the sunshine makes the fog glow like soft downy feathers gathered in my lovely valley. The presence of the Greedy Giant Mountain looms large and prevents the mist from leaving the area as he reclines across the landscape.

Hugging the hills, I spy the spooky limbs of bare trees, their fallen leaves spreading a deep golden carpet that will protect and nourish the land over wintertime. Nature is in retreat as daytime shortens and small creatures snuggle-up to sleep.

On the mountains a broad, trodden pathway follows the crest up and down the ridges, imprinted by centuries of humble-beings plodding their way. Heather is showing pink around the amazing shapes of huge circular and square markings that can only be seen from above; perhaps carved by that sleeping, greedy giant, displaying a menacing warning to a passing dragon like me.

Nearby is a special place, where long ago stood a ring of ancient rocks, huge and powerful and carefully sited to overlook Distant Lands, their purpose unknown, but every now and again these mysteries can reveal themselves in the strangest of ways, as Gwillim the goat discovers.

Below me I see Posty's van and hear its TOOT, TOOT! as it reaches each little home in the valley. Folk appear from their stony places to chat, they exchange letters while commenting about the weather and some moan about the state of the roads. Posty knocks to see if old Mrs Thomas is up and hopes a cup of tea and slice of homemade cake is ready for him. Afterwards he trundles up the Jones' farm track, skilfully dodging their sheepdog's fangs by throwing her a handful of doggy treats.

Today I notice Posty has an extraordinary delivery in the back of his van – it is Gwillim the Goat wedged in between the parcels. Gwillim regularly escapes from Piggledy Farm up at Wendle-y-Way, which is found high in the valley. Last night he had nibbled his way down the valley road until Posty found him happily licking the paint off the leaning signpost pointing to the Crooked Village.

Gwillim belongs to Bertie Bristles, a recluse who doesn't like folk and if a lost tourist bothers him for directions, he mumbles his reply, "Well I wouldn't start from here if I were you!"

Kind Posty had coaxed Gwillim into his van with his endless supply of doggy treats and is on his way to return him to Bertie. He had not realised how smelly a damp old billy goat could be, especially from the extra fumes caused by his unusual eating habits.

Come fly with me to Piggledy Farm where we can meet Posty and Gwillim – hold on as we take a big leap. Can you see the Crooked Village fading into the distance as we travel along Narrow Ridge? We are passing The Darren and Shepherd's Fall, following the broad mountain pathway and moving on to Pilgrim's Crossing, where tracks from Tumble Towers and Distant Lands meet. Look, there be a rambler waving his walking stick over on Tups Tump – do you think he's seen us? Now we can race up the straight trail of Crow's Way, but be careful to stop before Bleak Boulder Pass – beyond here only brave sheep and tough little ponies dare to live.

Wendle-y-Way lies below us, its few homes are scattered about while the little prayer places hide in sheltered nooks by the winding brook. Many dwellings are abandoned and unwanted, as this area is considered to be too remote, being far away from the busy lands. This isolation seems to breed independent, strong-minded characters, so it is no surprise to find that in his rambling hillside farm, Bertie Bristles prefers to exist alone.

Piggledy Farmhouse is really rundown, with roof tiles slipping and window frames splitting. The outside toilet has 'Ty bach' marked over its doorway, inside a raised stone base with a wide wooden toilet seat covers a deep pit – for it is not the flushing type. On the yard, Wesley the sheepdog hears Posty's van toot as it comes up the long farm lane, returning Gwillim...

Posty was relieved to be on the steep track to Piggledy Farm, Gwillim had been kicking his hooves against the rear doors for the last five miles and Posty did wonder what sort of mischief he was up to. Gwillim had indeed sampled a few of the postal packages; one contained large cotton pants for Mrs Powell while another had black inky stuff for Mr Fleecroft's printy-thing. Gwillim didn't enjoy tasting either of them and felt quite ill. Posty opened the van doors and he gingerly jumped out to reveal his black-stained face with soggy parcel string dangling from his mouth.

His owner Bertie had small, round, green eyes that peered out from his mass of hairy white bristles, while on top sat a Dai cap hiding his hairless patch. He didn't say much and just sucked in air irritably when seeing Posty with his devious goat. But, Gwillim was useful at keeping visitors away – the locals never came near the crafty goat, as he would chase and butt. Sometimes at night he would escape and hide behind a bushy branch that over-hung the tiny church wall; when folk came along he would poke out his white bony face and frighten the poor souls away.

Bertie grabbed Gwillim by his horns and dragged him over to the orchard, ignoring Posty. Posty frowned and thought he wouldn't bother returning Gwillim next time and promptly gave Wesley the sheepdog all of Bertie's letters to chew instead of his usual treats.

Gwillim trotted over to the leaning apple tree with its trunk stripped bare of bark by all his nibbling; underneath rested an old green Forestry van. This rusting heap was bought as scrap years ago for the price of a couple of ciders – its back doors were fixed open so Gwillim could shelter inside. The front seats were eaten down to their springs and the steering wheel chewed as if a huge rat had gnawed around the edges. The tyres had their treads munched off and the bodywork was faded where the paint had been licked away – Gwillim had certainly kept busy, trying to satisfy his greedy habits.

Bertie Bristles retrieved his soggy, bitten letters from Wesley and returned to his neglected house. In the kitchen was a large wood-burning stove that often puffed out smoke when a gust of wind blew down the chimney, making the place smell of woody fire.

His old oak table was littered with mugs, pens, letters and papers; Bertie reached for the nearest mug and winced as he gulped down a mouthful of yesterday's unexpectedly cold tea. His armchair was draped with an old blanket and this was where Bertie sat alone each evening.

The cosy kitchen was now the only dry place left in the farmhouse. Unable to afford the repairs to the roof, Bertie had steadily moved out of every room, until he only lived and slept in this one remaining space.

The evenings darkened quickly at this time of year. Bertie finished his outside duties, feeding his sheep, checking the pigs and not forgetting to shut the hens up in case Foxy called. He secured his sheepdog to a rope in the porch and gave him his meal. Bertie retired for supper with a bottle of his homemade cider – while Gwillim plotted yet another escape!

The old goat sniffed the rusty latch of the orchard gate; flicking it up with his nose, the gate swung open. He ambled around the farmyard finding different tastes until he reached the outside toilet, Ty bach – meaning 'little house' because that is what it was. Gwillim went into the dark and spidery room and found the toilet paper, he tugged at the dangling sheets until the roll spun out of control, unravelling all over the floor. He jumped onto the wooden bench over the toilet pit and settled himself down, his big belly rested nicely into the hole of the toilet seat.

Bertie swiftly brushed his few teeth over the kitchen sink before sliding the big kettle on to the hot stove ready for his wash. Keeping to his routine he ventured outside to the toilet, knowing his way in the darkness, he entered the little house. Well, I don't know who was most surprised when Bertie sat right on top of his goat – Gwillim nearly plummeted through the toilet seat hole, while Bertie struggled to escape, stumbling over his trousers that were wrapped around his ankles.

3-7 The Tiny Church

Gwillim charged down the field feeling pretty flushed from his humiliating experience. He found the broken fence in the hedge where he always escaped, but tonight it was sewn up with knotted orange twine and looked like a giant spider's web. Impatiently he stomped up and down the boundary until he remembered a place where he regularly returned home, over the wall of the Church.

Following along the hedge Gwillim found the tiny whitewashed church and gracefully jumped over the wall into the graveyard. The thick scented yew trees created a spooky setting, the windows of the church watched like dark staring eyes while its pointed bell-tower tilted slightly like a witch's hat. Nearby the owls hooted to each other asking, "Hooow are yooou?" as they awoke for the night.

Gwillim nervously stepped around the headstones, not to wake any mischievous spirits; he quickly trotted to the gap in the wall and squeezed through, then tiptoed along the path on to the valley road – he felt the church watching him – until he was safely over the little stone bridge.

The greedy goat was getting hungry; he could see a cluster of tents in a meadow nearby and could smell the lingering waft of food and thought what treats might be in store for him there – the lure of chewy canvas and nibbledy rope seemed very tempting.

As Gwillim neared the camp he could hear the excited giggling girls of Sparrow Patrol as they munched away on their midnight feast.

"Anyone for crispy porkers?" offered Annabel, in the tent.

"Yuck, that's pig's skin!" retorted Hannah, "I'll keep to my low calorie bites, fank you very much." Molly laughed smugly and then pulled out a large tin from under her pillow. All torches shone on the container as the lid was lifted, revealing a big yummy chocolate cake.

"Wicked!" cried the girls. Poor Amy pulled her sleeping covers over her head and begged for them to be quiet, "I don't feel well," she moaned.

The girls tucked into the cake, Rosie grabbed her can of fizzy drink, pulled back the opening ring and sprayed the quarters with sticky juice.

Molly suddenly signalled to the others to hush, her dark eyes widened with fear as something stirred outside. The girls panicked as the tent shook, they screamed at the tops of their voices when Gwillim tugged violently at the canvas side until he was able to rip off a chunk.

Group leader Miss Marshall swooped into the tent wearing her flowing nightdress. "Calm down girls, whatever is the matter?" she demanded.

Sparrow Patrol quickly hid their goodies under their pillows and craftily answered altogether, "Nothing Miss."

Gwillim sneaked off unseen, to digest his strange tasting scrap.

In the morning mist the five members of Sparrow Patrol assembled wearing waterproof clothing and chunky walking boots, they had large bags strapped on their backs and shiny charts dangling from their necks.

The girls complained of feeling tired and poor Amy wobbled weakly under the weight of her load; they were the first of the groups to set off on their trek over the mountains to gain their Outdoor Pursuits badges.

Miss Marshall reminded them of the Mountain Rescue emergency drill. "Don't forget, six blasts on your whistles or flashes on the torch, but leave a minute's pause before repeating it – pay attention, Hannah!" she snapped, as Hannah dreamily twiddled with her hair.

"But Miss, my hair is curling up in the damp wefer," she whinged, while the others sniggered quietly – except for Amy.

Annabel interrupted, "We could always shout six times, Miss."

"I'm glad someone in Sparrow Patrol has a brain, now off you go and don't forget to shut all the gates behind you," instructed Miss Marshall.

The girls dissolved into the mist, Amy was last, dragging her feet as they left camp over the meadow stile. Well it all began badly for Rosie, the little track was so slippery, it was almost a small stream and she slipped face down into the mud. Amy had to smile when Rosie was pulled to her feet looking as though she had been dipped in chocolate.

The mist thickened into fog making it hard for the girls to see their way, but Molly took charge and ordered them to keep close and follow her. They climbed over a stone-stepped wall and proceeded across the meadow until Annabel whispered uneasily, "What if there's a bull in this field?" Sparrow Patrol stopped and nervously clung on to each other, listening expectedly for the sound of thundering hooves.

"Now what do we do?" Rosie frowned, cracking the mud on her face.

"Run!" shouted Molly and the girls scattered to the edge of the meadow.

After finding their way along the hedgerow boundary they managed to regroup at a gate. They studied their maps but already found themselves lost and decided to continue down the track. Then a big stone structure loomed into view, an eerie sight – the girls felt compelled to touch the crumbling stone and wondered what the arched building used to be.

"It's an old monastery," declared Annabel finding it on her map, "so we must go this way," and she walked into the fog. Amy wearily got to her feet after resting and felt she must have caught her brother's recent ailment of Chicken Pox. She shouted to her pals, but the girls had disappeared from view. Pitifully, Amy called again, "Somebody, please help me," then miraculously she saw through the mist a divine apparition, a beautiful white lady floating serenely – but she pointed two ways.

Amy fell to her knees in awe at this magnificent sight until Annabel and Molly found her and pulled her to her feet.

"Come on, no time for praying, let's get going," insisted Molly, as they dragged her passed the old monastery's marble statue of the Virgin Mary. The girls linked arms and continued their journey laughing and joking about Amy's confusion. They turned down a dark, narrow cutting, edged with spiky hawthorn and wispy blackberry; the pathway was carpeted with golden leaves as deep as a sheep's knee and the girls waded through the foliage kicking at the crispy scraps – what a lovely noise they made!

Hannah noticed the clusters of blackberries clinging to their prickly brambles. "Lush," she enthused, carefully picking a handful and tossing them into her mouth, but, "Yuck!" she spluttered and spat them out – not knowing by this time of year the witches have breathed on them turning them sour; they all giggled at Hannah's reaction to the bad taste.

At the end of the pathway Sparrow Patrol rested on a fallen tree; Rosie retied her boots while Molly offered her squashed chocolate cake around. Amy, looking pale just drank her water. Then a strange shuffling noise could be heard, 'Scrunch, Scrunch!' The girls listened anxiously, was someone following them? Quickly, Sparrow Patrol gathered up their things and fled down the hill, until they reached the valley road.

Following in the tracks of Sparrow Patrol, Gwillim skipped along the leafy pathway in a weirdly cheerful mood. Flicking his hooves through the leaves, he smiled at the imaginary owl that sat in the hawthorn and bragged to him, "I can fly up to the highest branch too!" He saw a giant rabbit race pass and declared that he could run faster than the fastest creature in the valley and attempted to show his fantasy friends his agile abilities but ended up tripping over a stone. The clumsy goat staggered to his feet without a worry and seemed to be under a silly spell – perhaps the effects of eating that scrap of canvas tent?

After finding the valley road, Gwillim tried to follow the scent of Sparrow Patrol; with his nose in the air he strutted along the middle of the lane unaware of the line of traffic tooting behind him.

At last he turned up the track to Tups Tump and surprisingly ignored a line of ramblers that he normally would have bothered. He ambled by the garden of Bluebell Farm and noticed, in double vision, the familiar tatty sight of Squawk the Scarecrow, who now leaned redundantly against a shed. Gwillim stared cross-eyed at his tasty chum, but today instead of nibbling at his straw, Gwillim just grinned and continued on – pursuing the drifting washing line of clothes flapping in front of him, like a kite charming him up the mountain. He was certainly in a peculiar mood.

The girls of Sparrow Patrol made good progress on their trek but had not realised that poor Amy had trailed so far behind that she had totally lost her way in the fog. Unwell and exhausted, Amy sat on a rock and felt her brother's spots erupt on her face, they were very itchy and she began to sob – but then she heard a plodding sound approaching.

"Hannah, Molly, is that you?" Amy sniffed and looked up through her tears to see the fuzzy white figure of Gwillim emerging from the mist. It scared her to her feet and she quickly climbed up the mountain as fast as she could, hoping to catch up with the other girls of Sparrow Patrol.

Amy began to feel faint and while wandering aimlessly she did not detect Gwillim creeping up behind and nibbling at her bag. Ripping a hole, he steadily pulled out Amy's things – tissues, gloves, chocolate, torch, thick socks and yum, yum, canvas shoes with tasty laces – until the naughty goat made a trail of her items along the mountainside.

As her bag got lighter Amy was able to walk faster until she found herself above the hazy mist and on the sunny slopes of the mountaintop, the landscape looked beautiful with pink heather and grazing sheep. Still in a happy mood, Gwillim skipped behind with a toothbrush hanging from his mouth following Amy who dreamily paced on as if under a powerful spell until she stopped, turned and continued to the crest of the mountain.

Amy and Gwillim soon reached the edge of my patch, where the endless sight over Distant Lands is found. Just here, between the heather, is the grassy area where once existed the ancient circle of standing stones. Situated in the middle was a large flat rock, Gwillim quickly jumped upon it and skipped about as though he was the king of all the creatures.

Amy was hot and drowsy and sat herself down at the edge of the circle; she leaned back on her bag and closed her eyes. Gwillim tucked his legs under him and settled down; soon both souls drifted off into deep sleep.

Molly, Hannah, Rosie and Annabel eventually realised that Amy was not with them. "We must go back and find her," ordered Molly, "we should stick together," and the girls agreed to follow the track back along the mountaintop in the hope of finding Amy.

Later, as night approached, a strange thing happened, I could not believe my dragony eyes for around that circle where Amy and Gwillim slept, appeared those huge great stones from years ago.

Gwillim awoke from his slumber with bad tummy ache – he was sure it was from eating all his unusual scraps – then he noticed the enormous rocks that were surrounding them. He tried to stand up but, sensing a rope tightly binding his legs together, Gwillim went into a panic and bleated loudly over to Amy, "Naah Naah, waaaake uuuup, Naah Naah!"

Hearing a loud harsh cry, "Ow do yoou like it, aw tied up!" Gwillim looked around in confusion trying to find the threatening company, but he could only see Amy who was still fast asleep.

"I'm over 'eeer," shouted the sinister voice. Gwillim watched nervously, then from behind a large stone it called louder, "But I'm really eeeer!"

The worried goat turned his head to see the raggedy image of Squawk the scarecrow; he chuckled spitefully making his old sack face crease and his button eyes squint in evil contemplation. Gwillim blinked and wondered if he was really seeing things? He had never seen Squawk like this before, not even when he had cruelly devoured his stuffing.

The scary scarecrow, somehow leapt about with his legs twined together, taunting the greedy goat – Gwillim recalled the many times he had pulled out Squawk's straw while the crows above chortled, "Haw, Haw!" as he comically collapsed from his post – now the crows laughed at him, "Haw, Haw!" until Gwillim bleated back, begging for forgiveness.

Meanwhile, the other girls of Sparrow Patrol stumbled through the heather looking for Amy, having lost their way in the dark. They could hear the faint calls of Gwillim and see in the distance the stones lit up by the moon but imagined them to be a spaceship – landed on the mountain – and excitedly ran to get a closer look.

The wonderful sight of the standing stones was a vision that once graced the landscape many years ago; the smooth purple rocks were patterned with white lacy lichen that had been created by centuries of Welsh weather. Long shadows from these huge towering structures stretched like fingers pointing over the rolling heather, maybe indicating an important location. Placed by humble-beings of long ago, was the ring of standing stones trying to tell us its secret meaning?

A peculiar feeling flowed over the area making Gwillim feel uneasy. He cautiously looked for Squawk the scarecrow and was thankful he had gone – but while one chilling event had passed another was about to happen.

Stepping into the circle Amy appeared clutching a spear and dressed in skins. She danced around Gwillim, howling a strange song with a repetitive beat and stared at his large tummy, pointing to the moon with her spear. The horrified goat knew he was the fattest beast about and feared something terrible was going to happen to him, but he could only blame himself for being such a greedy goat.

The great standing stones seemed to grin at him like a mouthful of crooked teeth, Gwillim vowed to himself, "Okay, I will not consume any more naughty stuff, especially not scarecrows – I'll only eat grass, just like the sheep doooo!" and he bleated again so he might be saved.

3-16 The fattest Beast about

3-17 Vision on the Mountain

The moon moved and its glow shone around a large stone and glinted on Gwillim's head, Amy stepped nearer in her hairy animal skins and Gwillim worriedly imagined that his huge coat would fit a whole tribe. She danced about him, but oddly enough, her painted face had not a spot to be seen – Gwillim moaned desperately, wishing all would be well again.

Thinking it was an alien craft, Sparrow Patrol advanced towards the vision of the standing stones, but to their disappointment it began to disappear into the landscape. They decided to continue along the sheep's trail winding in the direction of Gwillim's bleating and eventually found the noisy goat. Shining their torches about, they were amazed to discover Amy, who was still asleep. "Look at her spots!" shrieked Hannah and they shook her until she awoke. Amy was delighted to see her friends again.

"Are you alright Amy?" they asked, "we've been looking everywhere."

"We even saw a UFO around here, but it disappeared," added Annabel.

"We heard that bald sheep on the rock over there," commented Rosie.

"I think that's a goat," laughed Molly, "and I wish it would shut up."

"What should we do now?" asked Annabel.

"Blow on our whistles six times," remembered Hannah.

"I think the goat's making too much noise, to be heard," assumed Molly.

"Give us your scarf Amy," requested Hannah, "I have an idea."

Poor Gwillim woke abruptly with bright lights dazzling him, as dark images gathered around. One shouted, "Hold his horns!" and a firm grip tugged his head sharply. Gwillim felt a muffle being tied around his nose; he braced himself as he regretted being the greediest goat in the valley. The gag was loosened so he could call six times – the girls repeatedly tightened the scarf around Gwillim's nose to stop him bleating and then let him again do another six loud bleats.

What a comical sight – the girls were certainly a smart lot.

Then out of the darkness torch lights appeared and the girls screamed with delight as the local Mountain Rescue team and their dog approached. Gwillim felt a strap tighten around his neck and was glad to find he could stand up again, but he had such a bad head. He noticed the big stones had disappeared and Amy was back in her walking gear, while the others chatted non-stop to the Rescue beings.

With great relief, Gwillim realised everything seemed normal again and was happy to be led down the mountainside, following the Rescue team and Sparrow Patrol with Amy wrapped up warm. Pippin the Rescue dog ran about wagging her tail proudly – having 'sniffed out' Amy's trail of items up the mountain – but it was really Gwillim's cries that alerted the team to find them in that special place.

Voices crackled from the talk-y-things – where everyone was called Roger, and then Gwillim heard a familiar voice, "Fancy Gwilly the billy coming good," called Posty from the front of the group.

Gwillim, "Naahed," backed to Posty, who is a part-time rescuer, and was hopeful of being returned to Piggledy Farm just like all the other times.

Bright lights advanced over the ridge and others joined the party as they made their way back to the Crooked Village.

"Best get the girls to a warm place," suggested one of the team.

"They'll be fine with a hot drink and a bit of rest," said another.

"We've got to get the girls back to Wendle-y-Way, so why don't we ask Mr Bristles if we can stop at his place?" enquired another.

"I knows 'ees got a good hot stove for a kettle," piped up Posty, "but 'ee may take some convincing," and they agreed to try.

Soon they reached their motors where Miss Marshall was worriedly waiting for them all; she hugged Amy reassuringly. The big metal rescue motor was painted up with colourful stripes and the rescuers reloaded their bits and pieces into the motor and tied the big stuff on the roof.

Gwillim looked for the post van but it was nowhere to be seen, Posty got into another motor and shouted from the window, "Someone else can take the old goat back!" and zoomed away adding, "see you up there."

They decided to get Gwillim into the big Mountain Rescue motor and the girls laughed when it took four of the Rescue-beings to heave the stubborn old goat into the back with them and Miss Marshall.

The Mountain Rescue vehicle whizzed up the valley road and they all chuckled at the bad smell from Gwillim; Pippin the rescue dog growled each time the hungry goat sniffed her. At last they turned up the track of Piggledy Farm, Bertie's place had a welcoming glow from his kitchen window, while wisps of smoke drifted from the chimney.

Wesley barked furiously at the advancing motors invading his farm. Bertie angrily opened the kitchen door to watch in dismay the parade of uninvited vehicles trespassing on his land. He ordered Wesley to 'see them off' while he returned inside slamming the door behind him — he really doesn't like other folk.

Posty knocked on the kitchen door and called, "Come on Bertie, we've brought your goat back, don't you want to hear what he's been up to?" The others stood close as Wesley circled them, but the girls urged the sheepdog over and he wagged his tail and licked Amy's spotty face.

"Have a heart Bertie," pleaded Posty as he saw him watching from the window. Bertie tugged the curtains shut and slid the kettle onto the stove, the door squeaked open and he grumpily beckoned them in.

As Sparrow Patrol sat on the frayed mat in front of the stove, they noticed the bottom oven door was slightly open and could smell the big pair of muddy boots that were drying inside. The clutter strewn about the place fascinated them – they were the remnants of Bertie's family possessions, telling their story in his one remaining room.

A leather bridle hung from the curtain rail, once belonging to his last faithful horse Felix who dragged, heaved and carted all his lifetime serving the farm. The old pots on the shelves were once saved for jams and pickles – for Bertie's mother lovingly picked, boiled and filled them. The patched bedspread on his sleeping place was fondly stitched with scraps from clothing and curtains – he felt comforted with his things about him.

Bertie heaped tea leaves into his teapot and mumbled that he only had four mugs, but then he shuffled in his floppy slippers over to the cupboard and opened its doors to reveal a full set of best crockery.

Jim from the Rescue team tried to chat to Bertie asking, "Do you have a problem getting out when it snows?" There was a pause, and then Bertie frowned and answered, "Me, I don't go far, just to town, for Market." Justifying his question Jim added, "But you have such a long driveway." Bertie cleverly replied, "It has to be that long or it wouldn't reach the farmhouse," and he smugly laughed at his own joke until he coughed.

Amy scratched at her spots as she sipped her hot tea; Bertie looked on a high shelf and found a bottle with thick, white liquid, he twisted off the top and passed it to Amy. She sniffed it and attempted to pour it into her cup, but Bertie smiled kindly and said, "No, it's for your spots."

Realising her mistake, Amy let Miss Marshall rub the liquid over her face and soon she felt the soothing effect of the herbal potion that had often been used in the Bristles household.

The Mountain Rescue team enjoyed their welcoming drinks, they asked Bertie about the places and folk in the old faded pictures hanging around the room and he was proud to chat about his past memories.

The girls got restless and asked Miss Marshall if they could go out and see Gwillim. "Go on then, but don't get in to mischief," she allowed.

Sparrow Patrol shone their torches around the orchard, wildly looking for Gwillim; he winced as they approached thinking he might have eaten something he shouldn't, luckily he only had a belly full of grass.

Wesley and Pippin ran around as the girls talked about their dramatic adventure and how the fat goat had saved their lives. Later Bertie and Miss Marshall found the girls messing about with sticks, poking at a big heap of wood in the orchard and they called to their leader. "Miss, Miss, it's Bonfire night tomorrow, please, please, can we have it here?"

The next evening Bertie gathered more fallen leaves and branches, stacking them onto the heap of wood – he was going to make the best bonfire he could. Gwillim watched as he picked up all the rubbish around the orchard and hoped his owner wouldn't find any half-chewed forbidden things that he had stolen over the years.

The girls from the camp appeared carrying a funny looking scarecrow that they had made earlier – calling it Guy. Bertie helped them place him on top of the pile. Other invited locals, including some of the Mountain Rescue team, joined the party and brought goodies in their baskets.

Soon the pile was lit and it flickered and crackled as large flames danced through its structure making faces glow, Guy started to smoulder and the girls shrieked with amusement as he burned.

Rolls and cakes were shared around, Wesley and Pippin skipped about sniffing out fallen fodder on the ground. Bertie appeared with glasses of homemade cider and grinned to see the happy crowd enjoying themselves and wondered why he hadn't ever had others around before.
"Can we have the fireworks now?" asked Molly and soon the area was sizzling with bright cascades of sparkles and spinning flames.

Gwillim watched the flashing celebrations in his orchard and was pleased there were no loud exploding rockets that had once upset him.

Gwillim reflected on his adventure in the mountains and the strange time he had in the circle of stones, but was pleased to be back on his patch. He thought it would be a long while before he went off exploring again and making a nuisance of himself eating all sorts of rubbish. Then he noticed a smouldering firework pinned to his tree and quietly wondered if it might indeed make a tasty treat for breakfast.

It leaves me thinking, did Gwillim really learn from his eventful experience, did he actually travel back in time to reveal the secret of the standing stones – what do you think?

The girls of Sparrow Patrol gained their Outdoor Pursuits badges and were highly praised for their cleverness in raising help, but above all they couldn't stop talking about their apparent sighting of a visiting space ship.

So let this be a warning to walkers who tread the mountains above my lovely valley, if you stumble into a grassy circle amongst the heather – beware of its powers and step out quickly – or it might just present you with a challenging time?

Whatever the mystery, Sparrow Patrol returned safely, and amazingly Bertie Bristles discovered the joys of mixing with humble folk and was never lonely again.

.........................there's lovely.

Proper Dragon Tales

If you have enjoyed this book, you may like to visit the website at www.properdragontales.co.uk to see the other books and products available in this series. To join the mailing list and be informed of new releases please use the "contact caroline" puff or email her at downey@properdragontales.co.uk.

Caroline welcomes your comments or book reviews which can be submitted via the "book reviews" section of the website.

Next Book No. 4 Muds and Floods
Published Sept. 09

As wild storms rage over the Black Mountains, will the baby bunnies of Golden Glade Warren survive their watery journey down the rapids of the rising river?

Proper Dragon Tales

How to order Books and Prints
You may order directly from Caroline Downey
or via the Website. www.properdragontales.co.uk
Framed Canvas Prints are available from images in this book.
Please quote titles and code numbers when ordering.

No.1 'The Black Mountain Sheep' is an enchanting story of strange
happenings after the sheep were removed from the mountainside at
the time of the Foot and Mouth crisis. However it is a tale of hope
and regeneration told with lively dialogue by the Proper Dragon who
exists in his lovely valley.
Published Sept. 06

No.2 'Shadows in the Fforest' follows the capers of Larry long-legs
the naughty lurcher dog where he disrupts the peacefulness of the
valley. But he has a plan to put things right and he ventures with
Pickles the trekking pony into the woods where peculiar and wonderful
events send them deeper into the forest.
Published Sept. 07